Othello,
the Moor of Venice

Sweet Cherry
Publishing

Published by Sweet Cherry Publishing Limited
Unit E, Vulcan Business Complex,
Vulcan Road,
Leicester, LE5 3EB,
United Kingdom

First published in the USA in 2013
ISBN: 978-1-78226-075-2

©Macaw Books

Title: Othello, the Moor of Venice
North American Edition

Text & Illustration by Macaw Books 2013

www.sweetcherrypublishing.com

Printed and bound by Wai Man Book Binding (China) Ltd. Kowloon, H.K.

About Shakespeare

William Shakespeare, regarded as the greatest writer in the English language, was born in Stratford-upon-Avon in Warwickshire, England (around April 23, 1564). He was the third of eight children born to John and Mary Shakespeare.

Shakespeare was a poet, playwright, and dramatist. He is often known as England's national poet and the "Bard of Avon." Thirty-eight plays, 154 sonnets, two long narrative poems, and several other poems are attributed to him. Shakespeare's plays have been translated into every major existent language and are performed more often than those of any other playwright.

Othello: He is a general in the Venetian Army. He is a powerful figure, respected by all. He wins the heart of Desdemona because of his  virtues. But later in the play, he kills her because of his insecurities based on racial and cultural differences.

Desdemona: She is the beautiful daughter of Brabantio and wife of Othello. She appears meek, but is determined and confident.

Iago: He is an ensign to Othello and the villain of the play. He is manipulative, cunning, bold, and relentless. He is motivated for several reasons to take his revenge on Othello and Cassio.

Cassio: He is second in command to Othello. He is young and good-looking but lacks military experience. Iago resents his position in the military and uses him as a pawn to take revenge on Othello.

Othello, the Moor of Venice

Brabantio was one of the richest senators in Venice. He had a very beautiful daughter called Desdemona, whom all the men of Venice were crazy

about. But Desdemona always preferred the mind over the physical attributes of men— and these qualities could be fulfilled only by a black man called Othello, the Moor of Venice. Othello was very close to Brabantio, and during the many visits he had made to the senator's house, the lovely Desdemona had fallen in love with him.

But though Othello was a black man, the truth remained that there was no other like

him in the whole of Venice. He
had proved himself over and
over again in the several wars
fought between the state of
Venice and the Turks. He had
established himself as one of the
greatest generals the Venetian
Army had ever seen, and his
strategies of war spoke truly
of his intellectual acumen.

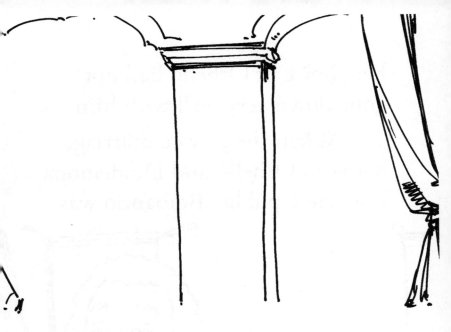

But though Brabantio was
well aware of the various good
qualities of the Moor, he was
not willing to have him as his
son-in-law. He had always hoped
that his daughter would choose
a senator or someone of nobler
rank, and definitely a white-
skinned man like himself. So

her choice of Othello had not
gone down very well with him.

When the private marriage
between Othello and Desdemona
was made public, Brabantio was

convinced that the black Moor
had used witchcraft on his poor
unsuspecting daughter and
tricked her into falling for him.
He declared that it was for this

reason that his
daughter had not
confided in him
and had eloped
with Othello.

But at that
time, there
was another
important matter
that also had to
be looked into.
News arrived that
the Turks had
once again laid

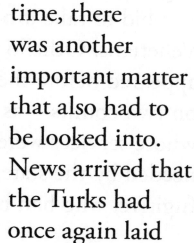

siege to the fortress of Cyprus
in a bid to take it back from the
Venetians. Othello therefore
appeared before the senate
on two counts—as a general
whose services were desperately
needed by the state, and also as a
fugitive, who had been charged

by Senator Brabantio for having abducted his innocent daughter.

Brabantio's age and seniority in the senate allowed him a hearing from the members of the senate present. But since he was so emotionally charged when making his accusations against Othello, the jury could not take him seriously. On the other hand, Othello merely recounted how he had won over Desdemona by telling her tales of his conquest and other stories whenever he visited Brabantio's house. The court came to the conclusion

that Othello had merely wooed
the noble Desdemona and that
could not be labeled a crime.

But even more in Othello's
favor was the testimony of
Desdemona herself. She appeared
in court and claimed that while
she was indebted to her father
for her life and education, she
had chosen to marry Othello

of her own accord. The court
now had no doubts about the
matter and the verdict was
clearly stated in Othello's favor.

Brabantio realized there was
nothing he could do but give
his daughter to the Moor with
his blessing. But in his state of
sorrow and misery, he told the
Moor, "Look at her, Moor, if
you have eyes to see with. She
has deceived her father and
she may deceive you as well."
So saying, Brabantio left.

Now it was time for Othello to set sail for Cyprus to deal with matters of the state. Desdemona, not wanting to be parted from her husband so soon after their marriage, asked if she could accompany him. Othello was only too happy to agree. Upon

reaching Cyprus, they were
told that a tempest had blown
away all the Turkish fleets, and
so the city was safe from any
foreign conquest. Othello was
pleased, as now he would have
more time to spend with his new
bride. Little did he know that
the war was just about to begin.

Along with Othello, Michael
Cassio had come to Cyprus to
face the Turkish invasion. Cassio
was one of the Moor's closest
friends—a valiant Florentine,
who was adept in charming
women off their feet. Any other
man would surely be jealous
of Cassio being around his

beloved, but Othello felt no jealousy, and had no reason to doubt either Desdemona or Cassio. So, when Desdemona

and Cassio spent time together,
laughing at Cassio's jokes or at
his various stories, Othello did
not give it a passing thought.

Othello had recently
promoted Cassio to lieutenant,
making him second in
command. This had not gone

down well with many of the
soldiers in the army, especially
Iago, a more senior officer, who
felt that the promotion should
have been given to him rather
than Cassio, a mere novice. It was
true that Iago hated Cassio, but
now he hated Othello even more.

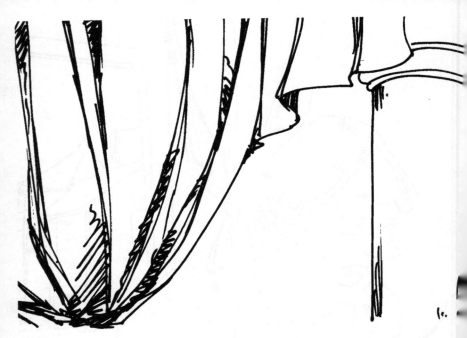

Iago's wife, Emilia, was
a maid to Desdemona and
learned that Othello was madly
in love with his wife. Iago
then started devising a plan,
which would simultaneously
generate the downfall of Cassio,
Othello, and Desdemona.

Now Iago was a shrewd
man and he knew that mental

anguish could cause a person
much more distress than
bodily torture; jealousy was
more powerful than the most

potent poison. He decided that if only he could prove to Othello that Cassio had been courting his fair wife, it might be reason enough for Othello to kill Cassio, or vice versa.

With the welcome news of the loss of the Turkish fleet, the whole island of Cyprus was

in a state of merriment. Wine was flowing in abundance and everyone drank a toast to Othello and his beautiful wife, Desdemona. It was during that night that Iago decided to put his plan into action. He had met a man called Rodriguez on the island, who was deeply in love with Desdemona and had been heartbroken to learn of her marriage to Othello. Iago knew that this man would perhaps be the best person to help him get things started.

That night, Iago first decided to get Cassio suitably drunk, knowing that he could not hold his drink. Then, with the connivance of Rodriguez, Iago got him to start talking ill of Bianca, a woman with whom Cassio was very much in love. Cassio, now considerably

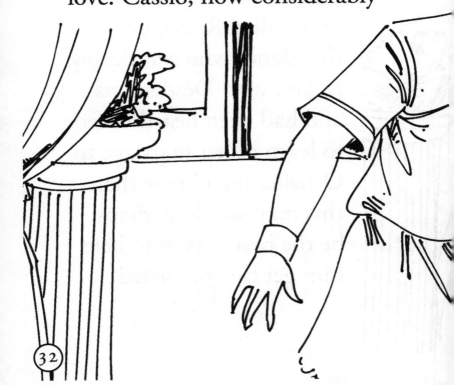

drunk, soon lost control of his
emotions and became embroiled
in a fight with Rodriguez.
Iago, whom Othello had put
in charge of maintaining peace
and order that night, tried to
stop them, but only managed
to spur them on further.

The ruckus brought Othello
out into the streets, and he
immediately wanted to know
who had started the brawl so that
he could mete out an appropriate
punishment to the guilty party.
But Iago, evil mastermind that
he was, tried to place all the
blame on himself, declaring to

the Moor that it was he who had been unable to stop the fight and so he should be punished. But finally, when it was learned that the guilty party was none other than his own lieutenant, Cassio, Othello was beside himself

with rage and at once banished
him, taking back his title.

Iago kept trying to intervene,
begging that Cassio be forgiven,
but Othello was so livid that
nothing could change his mind.
But in the process, Othello's
fondness for Iago grew and he

was pleased to see that Iago
had a sense of sacrifice.

Later that night, when Cassio
rued his actions before Iago, the
villain decided to take his game
to another level. He advised
Cassio that after marriage, wives
always have the upper hand over
their husbands. He therefore

told him to go and plead his
case to Desdemona, begging
her to help him get back in
favor with the general. Cassio,
thanking his esteemed friend,
decided to go to meet the noble
lady at once. Desdemona was
obviously shocked to hear
all that had happened that

night, and told Cassio that
she would definitely talk to
her husband about his case.

When the Moor returned
to his wife, she told him that
he should immediately forgive
Michael Cassio and reinstate
him to his previous rank.
Othello tried to delay the topic
to a later date, but the innocent

Desdemona would not have it. She was adamant that Othello talk to Cassio the next morning and not a minute later. Othello of course did not like this, but to keep Desdemona in good humor, he declared that he would do as she asked.

The next day, Desdemona called Cassio and explained to him what had taken place between her and Othello the night before, assuring him that he would soon find favor with the Moor again. Just as Cassio was leaving

after thanking Desdemona
for her efforts, Othello and
Iago entered the house. Upon

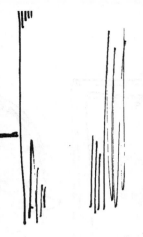

seeing Cassio come out of Desdemona's chambers, Iago mumbled, "I do not like that." Othello disliked what Iago was suggesting and immediately asked him the reason for his words. Iago again tried to defuse the situation by diverting the Moor's mind to other matters, but Othello would not give in.

Finally, after many excuses, Iago confessed that he did not enjoy seeing Cassio spend so much time with Desdemona. After all, the lieutenant was a young man and tales of his charm were well known in

Venice. However, he also
confirmed that Desdemona
was truly in love with her
husband and so Othello had
nothing to worry about.

Iago knew that he had sown
the seeds of jealousy in Othello's
mind. All he needed now was
some ploy by which to prove

to Othello discreetly
that Cassio was
indeed trying to woo
Desdemona, and that
his loving wife was
actually falling for
the young lieutenant.
And that chance
came rather soon.

Iago's wife,
Emilia, went to him
a few days later and showed
him a handkerchief she had
found, wondering if her husband
knew to whom it belonged. Now
Iago was a rather observant soldier,
and he at once recognized it as
belonging to Desdemona. As a
matter of fact, he remembered

that it had been a special present from Othello and that she was dearly fond of it. So he put his final plan into action at once.

The next day, when he met Cassio, he tried to cheer him up with tales of how Desdemona would see to it that he was back in favor with the Moor.

Cassio also tried to share his enthusiasm and hoped that things would work out for the best. Iago then urged him to spend some time with his beloved Bianca and forget about his troubles for a while. He gave him Desdemona's handkerchief and told him to give it to Bianca as

a gift, which would make her
love him even more. Cassio,
thinking that Iago was truly his
best friend in the whole world,
thanked him profusely and
set off for Bianca's quarters.

Later that day, when Iago
was alone with Othello, he tried

to talk to him about Cassio. He
told Othello that the young man
was most honorable and would
often give his beloved Bianca
gifts. Why, just the other day he
had seen him give her a beautiful
handkerchief, much like the one
the Moor had given Desdemona.

This immediately set Othello's mind racing as he wondered how the handkerchief that his friend mentioned could be the same as the one he had given to his wife.

The Moor told Iago of his suspicions, and though Iago tried to dispel his fears at first, he mentioned how Cassio had

been showing it off as a gift
from a beautiful lady. This raised
Othello's suspicions, and he
realized that his fair Desdemona
had been seeing Cassio and
exchanging love tokens with

him. Othello wanted to murder
Desdemona immediately, but
Iago convinced him to first see
if there was any truth in it.

So that night, Othello
decided to put the question
to Desdemona. Meanwhile,
Iago assured Othello that he
would arrange Cassio's death

and ensure that he never heard
of the vile lieutenant again.

When Othello went into
Desdemona's room that night,
he pretended to be unwell. He
asked for a handkerchief to
wipe his brow, and when she
gave him her own, he asked her
for the one that he had given

to her as a gift. She admitted
honestly that the handkerchief
was lost. But Othello then told
her that he knew she had given
it to Cassio as a token of her
love. Desdemona was distraught.
She could not believe that her
husband, the man she loved,

was accusing her of being in
love with someone else.

Othello was now convinced
that Desdemona was feigning
ignorance and trying to
divert his attention from
the matter at hand. Unable
to bear her dishonesty any

longer, he suffocated her
in bed with a pillow.

Emilia, who as usual had
gone to check if her mistress
needed anything before she
went to sleep, entered the room

and was the first to discover the gory murder. She started wailing, which alerted the guards. When they discovered the noble Desdemona dead, they were shocked when they realized

the culprit was none other than their general, the valiant Othello.

Othello lost no time in telling them what had happened over the past few days. He explained how Desdemona had been disloyal to him and that she

returned the love of Michael
Cassio. He also explained the
episode about the handkerchief,
but at this point, Emilia
entered. She told the people
present that she had found
the handkerchief and given it
to Iago. Othello realized that
Iago had been lying to him
about Desdemona the whole
time, and it dawned on him

that he had murdered his
innocent wife simply because
he could not keep his jealousy
in check. Unable to live with
his guilt, Othello drew his
sword and slit his own throat,
falling over the body of the
sweet Desdemona, dead.

Meanwhile, Iago had
been able to wound but not

kill Cassio, while Cassio had managed to elude the murderous Iago and drag himself, limping, to the court, followed all the way by his murderer. But as soon as Iago entered the room, the guards tried to arrest him.

Iago, looking at the people present, knew at once that his wife must have told them the story about the handkerchief. Without wasting another moment, Iago thrust his knife into his wife, killing her almost instantly. But though Emilia could not be saved, the guards arrested Iago at once. Later, he was charged with the murder of all three people—Othello, Desdemona and Emilia— and was sentenced to a most gruesome death. A fitting punishment indeed for the man who had killed the noble Othello and his treasured Desdemona.